Back-to-Front Bob

Also by Stephanie Baudet

A Present From Egypt
Double Bubble Trouble
In Someone Else's Shoes
M is For Mischief

Back-to-Front Bob

Stephanie Baudet

Illustrated by Derry Dillon

POOLBEG
FOR CHILDREN

Published 2003
by Poolbeg Press Ltd
123 Baldoyle Industrial Estate
Dublin 13, Ireland
E-mail: poolbeg@poolbeg.com
www.poolbeg.com

© Stephanie Baudet 2003

Copyright for typesetting, layout, design
© Poolbeg Group Services Ltd.

The moral right of the author has been asserted

1 3 5 7 9 10 8 6 4 2

A catalogue record for this book is available from the British Library.

ISBN 1-84223-039-5

Illustrations by Derry Dillon
Typeset by Patricia Hope in Times 16/24
Printed by
Nørhaven Paperback A/S, Denmark

For my sister Jan,
with love

Bob closed his gate and hurried up the street.

'Goodbye!' he said, greeting everyone with his usual cheerfulness. They all smiled and said hello.

They were used to Bob. He did everything back-to-front. His real name was Robert but spelt backwards it was Trebor, and that was the name of something else so everyone just called him Bob. That could be spelt backwards or forwards.

Bob wore his clothes back-to-front which made it very difficult doing up the buttons of his coat. He wore his trousers back-to-front, which caused problems too. And he wore his shoes on the wrong feet.

Usually Bob spoke the right way round, except when he was very excited, like today.

'Ev'I tog a boj ta eht ooz,' he said to his friend Pip, the milkman.

Pip laughed. 'You'll have to speak the right way round, Bob. I can't understand you.'

'I've got a job at the zoo,' said Bob, grinning. 'I start work at five o'clock and finish at nine o'clock.'

Pip frowned as he lifted a pint of milk from his cart. 'Don't you mean you start at nine o'clock and finish at five o'clock?'

'Yes, that's right, said Bob, shaking

his head. 'I must go or I'll be early.'
He hurried off towards the bus stop.

The bus squealed to a stop and the doors swished open. People nearly knocked Bob over as he tried to get on through a door marked *Exit*.

'To the zoo, thank you,' said Bob, struggling to get the money out of his back-to-front pockets. 'I've got a job there.'

6

'You be careful of those animals,' said the driver. 'Some of them are dangerous. I hope you know which ones are which.'

'Of course I do,' said Bob. 'Everyone knows that elephants have stripes and tigers have long trunks, but it's hippos I really like. All that black and white fur makes them really cuddly.'

The driver raised his eyebrows in surprise, but he knew Bob too.

When Bob got to the zoo he reported to the head keeper.

'Hello,' said the keeper. 'My name is Anna. I'll show you round and then you can start work. Here's a list of jobs for you to do.'

Bob looked at the list.

Feed fish to the penguins.

Let the zebras out into the field.

Hose down the elephants.

Clean out the chimps' house.

Anna gave him a tour of the zoo and then left him to do his jobs. He went and got the bucket of fish and took it to the zebras' stable.

'There you are,' he said. 'Here's your breakfast.' He held out a fish to one of the zebras but it turned away. None of them would eat their fish.

'Suit yourself,' said Bob. 'I've got lots of work to do.' And he went off to let the penguins into the field.

The field was some way from the penguins' house so Bob herded them along the road. All the zoo visitors stopped to watch and laugh at the penguins waddling on their little legs and Bob running from one side of the road to the other trying to keep them together.

At last they were in the field and Bob went to get on with his next job. He collected a bucket of water and a broom and went to clean out the elephants' house. That took quite a long time.

Three jobs done. One to go. Then he
could have his lunch. He was really
enjoying his work.

All he had to do now was . . .

He looked at the list.

Then he went to get the hose.

The chimps were in high spirits, swinging from the trees and putting on quite an act for the children watching.

Bob connected up the hose and turned on the tap. Water gushed out. He walked out into the chimp compound and aimed a stream of water at the nearest chimp.

LAOIS COUNTY LIBRARY

It seemed surprised at first and let out a great screech but then began to enjoy the cool water on such a hot day and chattered in delight. Soon all the chimps came to join in and the watching crowd laughed and clapped.

Suddenly the first chimp jumped
down from a tree, ran towards Bob
and in a flash he had snatched the
hose from Bob's hand and begun
spraying his friends AND Bob. Then,
as the crowd cheered, he turned the
hose on them too.

People squealed and ran away, and laughed, and came back. Then more and more people from all over the zoo came to see what all the noise was about.

Bob watched, not knowing what to do.

Soon someone else came to see what all the noise was about.

It was Anna, the head keeper.

She had found hungry zebras with their fish breakfast which they couldn't eat and the penguins in a field of grass which they couldn't eat either.

She had found elephants hot and dry and needing a wash down and now she watched the chimp with a hose spraying the crowd.

Anna was very cross.

Bob saw her cross face. He had made a mess of things, hadn't he? He had got things back-to-front as usual. Now he might lose his job and he was enjoying it very much.

He went and turned off the tap. The chimp looked at the end of the hose with surprise and then poked a finger into it to see if he could find the water.

The crowd laughed. Then he put the
hose to his eye to see where the water
had gone. The crowd roared.

At last it was five o'clock and time
for Bob to go home.

'How did you get on?' asked the
bus driver.

Bob just smiled but didn't say
anything. He was really worried.

Next morning when he arrived at
the zoo, there was a long queue waiting
for the gates to open.

He went straight to Anna's office and knocked on the door, his hand shaking.

'How did you think your first day went, Bob?' asked Anna.

Bob hung his head. 'I got things back-to-front,' he said.

'Yes, you did,' she said. 'The zebra were not too pleased with the fish to eat and penguins do not usually eat grass. The elephants had very uncomfortable dry skins too. But,' she smiled, 'the chimps really loved playing with the water and, the people did too. Have you seen the crowd here today? Word has spread that we have a new attraction. We haven't had so many visitors for a long time. I would like you to hose down the chimps twice a day during the summer holidays. Any other jobs I want you to do I'll tell you one at a time. Then you can't get them back-to-front.'

Bob smiled as he left her office and went to get the hose. He hadn't lost his job but he must really try to get things right in future.